To

Pony Castle

Published by Metatron
www.onmetatron.com
305-5555 Ave. de Gaspé, Montreal QC H2T2A3

ISBN 978-0-9939464-4-8

Editing | Guillaume Morissette
Layout and book design | Ashley Opheim
Cover art | Flora Hammond

First edition
First printing

PONY CASTLE

SOFIA BANZHAF

Metatron
Montréal

1.

We drown a dozen oysters in Kir Royales and sweet Chardonnay and I can tell by the rose colour of Kurt's cheeks that he is about to say something mean. It's not his fault. It's because we've been drinking since 3 pm. It's because we do that - start drinking at 3 pm. I don't tell him that I'm about to order another round of drinks. Kurt is looking at me with this flush in his cheeks and he is about to say something mean and sometimes I wonder whether I've successfully drained the affection out of him because I do that, I have a talent for these kinds of things, draining things, sucking things dry, and I know Kurt is about to tell me something because I asked him to, in my own quiet way. And so I go to the bar instead and I feel like I might just stay there, forever ordering more drinks, looking at him from the bar, buried in his coat pocket trying to find his crumbling hash cookie. Because the truth is when we aren't fucking, we don't make a very good pair and it makes sense that we aren't a couple, it makes sense Kurt gets that color in his cheeks, it makes sense that I have a boyfriend at home.

2.

Château Chevaux is full of hair. There are two cats and our plastic Barbie pony is propped up on the broken 1970's television set. The plastic pony has a tail of synthetic hair. The cats play with the tail. The pony has alopecia. The pony's name is Bunny. There is me and there is my roommate. We both have long hair. Sometimes I find a hair in my mouth and I pull on it and it turns out it was all the way in my throat and I pull for a long time and try not to breathe. My roommate has black hair. Really black. Like marbles or oil. She walks around in gym shorts and she mutters to herself. She has psoriasis. She leaves halved rotting peaches and limes around the house - just leaves them around. She told me that she had a psychotic episode when she was living in France. She is French. She told me that her psychotic episode involved a fruit stand collapsing. Involved her mother losing a tooth. Involved thousands of Euros going missing. I said, move in with me. I said, you seem nice, move in with me. You brought me cupcakes, move in with me. So now whose fault is it that I live with a muttering French girl. It's my fault.

We have hair and it clogs the shower drain. We are girls and our hair clogs the shower drain. It turns our showers into baths for small animals, for rodents.

My roommate knows about cheese. She is French and she knows some things about cheese. She knows about Morbier. She knows about Brillat Savarin. She knows about St. Felicien. She talks about cheese and now I know about cheese. I made her pasta with blue cheese and she didn't finish it. I don't know that much about cheese.

3.

I do this thing now where I go to Niagara to see my Omi for an afternoon and eat her Jell-O trifle and scoop some pearly white Percocets, Anita tells me. I crush them and soak them and strain them, she says. It's good for my liver. She is waving around her jingling jangling ice and vodka. She looks like a bankrupt heiress from the 20's, sitting cross-legged on my bed, bob cut and long fingers. She used to put one of those down my throat in high school, back when we were helping each other throw up for months before prom. We ate caffeine pills for lunch and knew the names of 70-90% of the f/w runway models.

We are supposed to go to a party. My roommate is mopping the floors outside my door - yes she is - the first time I have ever witnessed her cleaning and it smells like dewy lemongrass meadows. We can't go out there, I say. We can't pull 'a little princess' and walk across the shiny clean hardwood, I say. Anita seems relaxed. Let's paint our nails and draw little pandas with ice cream spluttered on their tiny bellies, she suggests. Let's cancel life.

4.

My boyfriend is sleeping in his bed and I have opened
the door and closed it behind me and am standing
there looking at him. The room smells like his nap
has already gone on for too long, like over the course
of his nap, his sheets have gotten dirty and now need
washing. Like the water in his cup has gotten stale
and the orange rinds on his plate gone moldy. I am
drunk on water kefir. I lower my backpack on the
floor, it's filled with carefully wrapped packages of
gleaming meat that I bought from my butcher. My
butcher has a new assistant, Lenny. He is 20 and tall
and his eyes shimmer like wet rocks on a riverbank
and when I asked him how to prepare the marinated
rabbit, I thought about his dick in my mouth and I
started to get that way that I get. And I kept looking
at him. And I'm sure my lips were plump. And I'm
sure he felt the small animal inside him rouse. And I
got on my bike and a little while later walked into the
house of my sleeping boyfriend. And I'm peeling
away the blanket from my sleeping boyfriend's body,
slipping off the boxer shorts he is wearing and he is
moaning a little bit, he is moaning a little bit more a
little while later, he is awake now, and he doesn't know

that the grin that I grin after I swallow is because he was someone else entirely for me and nobody can punish me.

5.

We are lying on brown grass in what's called a 'parkette.' The kind of park that's a strip of grass and a bench in the middle of two heavy traffic streets. Anita is grinning at me with her glossy brown eyes, a small metal case perched on her hand, arm outstretched to me. The clouds are moving and the shadows falling on her face make me feel like I am watching time lapse around her.

What's this, I say.

The metal case she's holding has small winding flowering plants engraved in it and I think about another case, one with my milk teeth in it, lost somewhere in my parents' basement in a box labelled VARIOUS. I think about how tiny the teeth were and I feel sad suddenly, the way I always feel sad when I think about the smallness of my child body.

Anita watches me open the case, watches me understand what's inside for the first time.

My pillbox, she says. Formerly known as my jewelry box. Rest in peace.

6.

I've got a croissant. I've got a poppy croissant at my house. Do you want it. It isn't too banged up. Charles is standing crookedly at the base of the steps leading up to Anita's apartment building. We are having a yard sale. We are selling her mother's Pierre Cardin cardigans and stacks of CDs and perfume we stole in high school. Do you want it, Charles persists. He's Anita's handsome crack addict neighbor. You're scaring the customers, Charles! Anita says. I tell Charles I will eat his croissant and he limps away. I look forward to the croissant.

Nobody else comes by for several hours, so Anita and I make up a game. It's called 'Swamp in the Belly' and it involves walking very slowly from one side of the street to the other. Whoever walks the slowest wins. It isn't easy. If you think it's easy, it isn't. It requires focus. It requires stamina, both physical and spiritual. What fucks you up is your wretched gut, making you lose your temper. It isn't easy.

In the middle of a game that I am winning, motor-cycle man pulls up noisily on his skeleton Triumph.

He lives a few doors down and we have never seen him without his helmet on. We have big dreams. We used to whisper feverish prayers for him to take his helmet off, but I've started hoping he never will. In fact, if I could have it my way, I'd have all men cover their heads with motorcycle helmets. If I could have it my way, they'd just have tiny eye holes and sunglasses on top. If I could have it my way, every man, everywhere, would be required to wear a head piece to cover their head. Don't fuck up my dreams, motorcycle man, I say, addressing the sky.

7.

Kurt and I have decided to go to the island. We pack a blanket and books and lie down on the beach and eat blackberries and I take photos of him and he isn't trying to run away. We smoke a little bit of grass and I feel okay about it. It's a good day. It's a nice time.

8.

The drug dealer's porch looks like a garbage waste-
land. Anita is looking at her phone and I am looking
at the flowerpot with cigarette butts. What are we
doing, I say to Anita, picking at the brown stump of
a plant. He will text us when we can come in, she tells
me a second time. I'm just trying to buy some drugs.
I'm not trying to live a complicated life, I say to
myself in my head. Anita's phone buzzes and she
says, okay, and she opens the screen door and someone
inside the apartment opens the door behind that and
we step into a narrow corridor and are led into a
bedroom that looks dark and small at first, but there
are well-watered plants, and his shoes are expensive,
I can tell. The drug dealer shakes my hand and doesn't
smile, but says his name and I say mine. He's slight,
my height, and has a smooth Asian face. He sits in
his computer chair and Anita and I sit on his bed and
I am suddenly worried. So what can I get you, he
says. There is incense burning somewhere and the
screen on his computer explodes into constellations
with every beat of the stressful drum and bass. What
did the hippie say when asked to get off the couch?
Nah-Ima-Stay, I joke. The drug dealer says, who is

this girl, still not smiling, but carefully deciding something about me. I am grateful to Anita who handles all our business including handing him 80 dollars more than I was prepared for. We shake hands again when we leave, he's an alligator lying in wait, we walk down the hallway, I turn around before I open the door, I say, keep the heart shining, and Anita says, okay now, and he says, you have to really pull on the door, and he says, enjoy those, and my fingers touch the little baggie in my pocket and I pull on the door.

9.

I am a virgin, pure and pale, stretched across my bed.
We called in sick, first her then me. There is fruit
scattered, the only thing I have energy to eat. Anita
is illuminated like only someone very wise can be.
She's stroking my hair and when she forgets every so
often, I jerk my body to remind her and she starts
stroking again, gently, like only someone very kind
can do.

Are you asleep, I say.

No, are you, she says.

A little bit, I say.

I'm happy, she says.

10.

My roommate calls me when I am in bed. She calls me when I am in bed, but it's not night, it's the afternoon. She calls me and she says what's up and her voice is weird. I say, what's up. She says, what are you doing. I say, I am working out to this work-out video. It's called 'Shred til You're Dead'. She says, cool. I say, what's wrong. She says, nothing. I say, what's wrong. She says, bad things are happening. She says, bad things are happening to good people. I say, really. She says, yes. Bad things are happening to good people because the planet is in retrograde. But soon the planet will move out of retrograde. And then good things will happen to good people. And bad people will try to stop good things from happening to good people. I say, am I good people. She says, shut up. Listen. She says, something is going on. Reality isn't real. There is another reality that is more real and we go there when we sleep. The soul, she says. I say, cool. She says, no, you don't understand. I have to do something. Things are bad. She says, you don't understand. My life has been orchestrated for this moment. I have to stop them, she says, you don't understand. I can control the sun.

11.

The first time I saw Kurt, he sat bleeding on a bench in a baseball field. Anita and I pressed against the chain link fence in our florals, sipping milkshakes. I knew what we looked like. I knew what we looked like, with the soft rain on us. And Kurt looked over and he saw what we looked like. And he looked away. We all went to a bar together after the game. Anita and this guy she was fucking, and me and Kurt and other guys from the team. Kurt ordered a beer at the bar. And I was already drunk because there'd been rum in our milkshakes. So I said, good game. I said, good game. He said, nah. He said, we lost. He said, my knee is bleeding. And a bird shit on me on my way there. I said, no way. Does that even happen. He said, it happened to me. He said, do you want a beer. I said yes. He put his hand in his pocket to get his wallet. I could see the outline of his cock. I could see this big bulge and I looked at it as he was counting money to give to the bartender to pay for my beer. And I looked at the nape of his neck when he gave the bartender his money to pay for my beer. And when he turned around, I took the beer and I looked at his eyes, and they were golden, like broken glass at the bottom of a pool, and he looked at me, and I said, hey, and I smiled, and I said, to sugar on our strawberries.

12.

I've got change in my palm and more in my pockets.
This jukebox belongs to me. This jukebox under-
stands me and God, too. I've been bought several
drinks. One whiskey cola by one man and three
vodka waters by a different man, the man I'm on a
date with. I say man because he is over 30. Seems
right. I'm on a date with this man and he has bought
me three drinks and I have bought him none. He's
sitting on a stool and has swiveled to watch me put
change in the jukebox. I can't concentrate on the
things he's telling me. I am thinking about the colony
of moths that has settled on my bedroom ceiling. I've
been watching the larvae cocoon and after some time,
a fully formed moth drops from the ceiling into my
bed. I'm not sure what to do about it. The man is
watching me, waiting for me to perform. What I feel
like could be happening but isn't happening at this
precise time, although in some ways has started
happening: I am cheating on my boyfriend and I am
cheating on the boy that I am cheating on my
boyfriend with.

What happens later is this: I am in this man's bed. Or should I say: This man puts me in his bed. Or should I say: We are high and he throws me on the bed. Or should I say: I take my dress off as soon as I am on the bed. Or should I say: I am told to take my dress off when he throws me on the bed. I am in this man's bed and my ass is in the air. And my back is arched. And the man likes it. I can tell he likes it. I am in this man's bed and it isn't 10 pm yet. But my ass is in the air and my back is arched. This is the part that counts. This is my time to shine. I am performing girl performing slut performing real person performing fantasy. It's a complex performance and I am very good. He says, tell me how badly you want this. I say, badly. He holds my throat and I make sounds like a dying bird at twilight. I can't help it. It's a complex performance and I am very good. I am so good that it becomes confusing. I am so good that I become the character. I am so good that when I walk home, I walk home as the character. I am so good that when I lie in bed, watching the larvae cocoon, burning myself with ashes from my cigarette, eyes heavy like diamonds, I lie there, unmoving as the character.

13.

The first thing I do when I get to the Dufferin Mall is take a dump, the first in days. Anita waits for me in the food court and when I come back, she's eating out of a box of fried chicken. We say nothing for a while, just eating. It feels good and it feels right to be here in this moment in time and space. Light streams in from the ceiling and illuminates the old men drinking apple juice out of cartons like a tableau. Teen girls dipping their hand in the fountain, flocks of boys experiencing brotherhood for the first time. And then there is Anita and me, picking at chicken bones, about to pawn her brother's Playstation 4 for 300 dollars and spend the rest of the weekend behind heavy drapes, playing Yahtzee with opiate eyes and listening to *The Jungle Book* in Hebrew on repeat.

How do you think your brother will kill you, I ask Anita as we leave the mall, wallets thick with twenties.

She turns to me. He can lick my dick, how does that sound, b.

14.

Mozart died from eating pork chops. The world is dangerous and my mother once told me that happiness comes from the heart, not the places you go and I say good, because I'm not leaving my room and I will draw circles in this notebook until my wrists break.

15.

Someone made notes in my handwriting on my post-its
and left them around my room.

Rather, it was me. Rather, I have been asleep.

The notes read:

stalactite dripping sounds cd

*my desire to be understood by others is the primary
way in which i introduce resistance and suffering
to my experience*

*wow look at that smoke stack. mother earth is a
poet for sure. oh yeah. a great artist.*

I look dully at the notes.

16.

I count backwards from 100.

I call in sick because I am sick.

Dude, not a good move, my coworker says on the phone.

I call Anita. What the fuck, I say. She says, yeah. I say, what should we do. She says, I don't know, I'm working on it.

I count backwards from 100.

17.

You are the sexiest woman in this city, he says. My boyfriend is trying to make me laugh.

He's blank like a dry-cleaned white shirt. He smells like men's body wash, men's moisturizer and men's deodorant. I am in his arms on his floor. I am crying like a child, but I am not a child. He says talk to me, talk to me. He sees me like this and massages my temples while looking directly at me, saying talk to me. How do you explain to someone that you've made an error, an error that involves the birth of them in your life and the birth of yourself. You focus on things and they expand, like stepping on a piece of gum on the sidewalk repeatedly. Squint. Think about your organs. Think about your pulsating heart when it was still palm sized. Think about clean blood and milk teeth. I won't make the same error a second time and that means I've grown. Isn't that the purpose of life, growth. Aren't I fulfilling my purpose.

Talk to me, he says.

I go into my boyfriend's bathroom and drink a bottle of Robitussin.

18.

When I was small, I would pick currants from the large towering bush in our garden. I'd bring them into the house and wash them, the sun from the kitchen window making them glow from the inside, like they were live things with veins. My mother would pour milk and sugar on top in a white porcelain bowl and I'd take a spoon and press the back of it onto a currant until it popped and I saw red swirl into the milk. I would watch the milk turn bright pink, slowly, like it was the sky.

19.

The flowerpot and butts have been removed. I am standing with my phone in both hands, staring at the glowing screen. I ring the doorbell. He's home and he will let me in, I say, my breath blooming on the window pane. A girl opens the door, she looks me up and down. It's for you, she yells into the house. I follow her inside, I go into his room, I sit on his bed and peel bills out of my pocket. Where's Anita, he says. On a trip, I say. I show him my money like a schoolgirl. I told you not to come here anymore, he says. I want to smile at him, tell him that I love him.

I don't have any more crushables, he says. I already told you.

I'll buy something else, I say. My mouth cracks in half.

20.

Kurt is young and he could lift me if he wanted to. I bled onto his bed, his Egyptian cotton sheets stained dark red in the shape of a butterfly. Very pretty, I think. Those sheets are expensive, he tells me from the balcony, lighting a joint, but of course he is lying. My period doesn't announce itself anymore. My body is living the life of a stranger's. Kurt is talking about his downstairs neighbor feeding raccoons, he could be talking to himself, he could be talking to anybody, his words float by me like anemones. I put my finger on the spine of the butterfly staining the sheet. I keep it perfectly still.

21.

It's 4 pm and my boyfriend is ordering us lunch at a Thai restaurant. I am punishing him for making me leave my house by withholding eye contact. He doesn't seem to notice, so I arrange for my sunglasses to slip down my head onto the bridge of my nose. When the noodles coated in thick sauce arrive, I poke around the plate like I'm over the idea of eating. In general. I feel elegant. You know what, he says. What, I say. I change my mind and pluck a cube of hard meat off my plate. I think we should go away some-where. Like a vacation, I say chewing. We can rent a cottage up north for a few days, he says. I say nothing. Then I say, who is going to pay for that. Now he's not so happy anymore. He's suddenly talking about very different things, and he isn't eating at all and don't you hate it when people have a full plate of food in front of them and don't eat any of it and just talk. So I eat for him, all my noodles, and when I reach with my fork to pierce one of his tiger shrimps, he grabs my hand and he says, are you listening, and the scene has turned into a scene, and I glance to see if anyone else is seeing this, and I say, excuse me, I have to use the bathroom and I stand up and walk through the restaurant, shaking only a little, his voice trailing behind me.

22.

I take a nap and let my arm dangle from the bed like a dead person.

23.

Kurt has tied a black string around my wrist. He says it will help me break bad habits. It's a shaman thing he learned from his pseudo-shaman friend who went to upstate New York for a retreat once.

Bad habits like what, I say.

Like anything you want. Smoking or, whatever, he says.

I take pleasure in how afraid he is.

I don't want to quit smoking, I say.

Happy birthday, he says, and gives me a furtive kiss on the brow like a brother.

24.

Ways to restore one's sexual appeal:

Smile at the subject to which you want to communicate your value as a sexual being as if they've broken open a crack in a cement wall with their bare hands and revealed a blooming flower.

Hunger in your eyes when you look at them, but appear to be practicing restraint - in other words, appear to smile, laugh, touch your hair, move *despite yourself.*

25.

A terrible idea, it dawns on me. A terrible idea to leave the city. We have been driving for hours, searching for this guy's 'farm.'

Does he actually live on a farm, I ask.

A terrible idea to trust that this guy has a bottle in a medicine cabinet with 167 white round pills that he doesn't need, and is giving away to us for free.

It's not a real farm, Anita says, chewing gum. She is driving, her eyes wide. She nervously touches the swinging rosary hanging from the mirror.

We pull into a dusty driveway, a bungalow in front of us, wheat fields around us.

We might die today, I say.

He's a nice guy, she says, applying lipstick in the mirror.

I don't think free drugs ever come from nice guys, I say.

Anita turns to me.

Oh, they aren't free, she says, and smiles like she's
drunk.

26.

I count backwards from 100, I get to 20.

The bedroom door swings open, laughter, Anita emerges, stuffing her blouse into her jean shorts. She says, let's go, and takes my arm, dragging me.

A man's voice: Hey, what about your friend? But we have slammed the car doors shut, the rosary quivers, Anita turns the ignition.

27.

The wheat field sways, a truck honks. We are between the reeds, she is counting pills, I am counting backwards from 100.

We should sell half, she says.

She has four pills in her hand, arm outstretched to me, her dark eyes glittering. She is melting into the horizon, becoming the setting sun, a grapefruit dripping.

I am queen of this life, I can do what I want.

I can say no. I can say anything I want.

The universe conspires to help, I have been told.

I count backwards from 100, I get to 95.

28.

My cigarettes are honeydew smooth. My stomach is empty. There is ice in my cola.

Anita is throwing up in the bathroom just like old times, but this is new. She took too much, she should have known. I hum the melody to "Orinoco Flow" by Enya loudly so she can hear it and feel comforted. She's moaning and muttering something. I open the bathroom door and she turns to me with red eyes and puke on her black velvet dress.

What do you need, I say.

She is barely awake.

This is heaven, she says. This is heaven.

29.

I come home and there are boxes everywhere. My French roommate is chewing on her fingernails in the middle of the living room.

What's going on, I say.

I'm moving today, she says. She looks at me and stops chewing.

Your nose is bleeding, she says.

No, it's not, I say.

Yes, it is, she says.

I see our plastic pony, Bunny, lying in a box.

Can you leave this here, I say, lifting it up to show her.

No, she says. It's mine, my friend gave it to me.

I'll give you money for it, I say. Eighty dollars.

Can anyone help you, she asks. Can you call anyone. Like your mom.

My French roommate is looking at me with big black eyes. She is wearing gym shorts and flip flops.

How much do you want for this, I say, holding the pony.

30.

I am queen of this life, I can do what I want.

I can stay here or go anywhere.

I can think of my mother, think of her face. The smell of her perfume, Opium by Yves Saint Laurent, ha ha ha. Her smooth feet, not like my feet. The books on her shelf and her birthday cards. Her high-pitched voice on the phone repeating my name. My milk teeth in a jewelry box in my bedroom, my 11-year-old braid we cut off and tacked to a cork board. The smallness of my child body, my child bones, my child heart.

Here are my freckles, look at how dense, like a wildfire consuming my face.

I am queen of this life.

31.

Kurt calls and says where are you and where have you been and this is not funny and do not hang up and he's a little boy playing man and I laugh and say, you know what, fuck collective consciousness, fuck Carl Jung and fuck Rothko, yellow and blue-yellow and blue

I can see the time spiral spiraling I can see backwards I am in the middle of two universes I am in the middle of everything I am above it and I realize everything

32.

There's a saying that drugs are hard to find when you start, but by the end, they follow you wherever you go, only it isn't a saying, it's just some person saying it once, one time, on *Intervention*.

r

33.

It wasn't Anita's fault. If you think it was Anita's fault, it wasn't. Because wasn't I the one who brought the small case with the engraved flowers. And wasn't I the one who watched her roll the pill between her fingers like a precious stone. And wasn't I the one who said, are you game or are you lame. And wasn't I the one that turned to her, hair wet with toilet water, bloodshot, muttering. It wasn't Anita's fault. But it wasn't my fault either. It wasn't a question of fault. That's an outdated model of thinking. It was just the way life snaked through us. It wasn't a question of fault. It was just that most things hurt and we didn't know why. It was just that we were confused. It wasn't that we didn't try. It was just that we wanted to feel more like water lilies. It was just that we wanted to feel more like water lilies on a Chinese lagoon.

Acknowledgements

Ashley Opheim & Guillaume Morrissette for their support & help & positivity & love.

Lynn Crosbie for her generosity & kindness.

Phoebe Wang for her insight & encouragement.

TO ORDER OUR BOOKS:
WWW.ONMETATRON.COM/SHOP

Sofia Banzhaf was raised in Germany and Newfoundland. She now lives in Toronto. *Pony Castle* is her first book, which was the winning title of the 2015 Metatron Prize for Rising Authors of Contemporary Literature.